BRUCE

Fun in the sun

£3.99

L 5/9

OTHER TITLES IN THE SAME SERIES

The Fat Cat!
0 7475 4235 X

Pax is always hungry! Whenever she smells something good to eat she just has to go and find it!

Pix the Hero!
0 7475 4240 6

Pix and Pax are always getting into trouble. But when Ben and Len are in danger, one of Pix's tricks comes in very useful!

Family Cats!
0 7475 4250 3

It is spring! And everybody is having babies – Betty Bird's chicks are about to hatch, and Bob the frog's tadpoles are growing very fast!

Fun in the Sun

LISA BRUCE

Illustrated by
Alison Carney

BLOOMSBURY
CHILDREN'S
BOOKS

First published in Great Britain in 1999
Bloomsbury Publishing Plc, 38 Soho Square, London, W1V 5DF

Copyright © Text Lisa Bruce 1999
Copyright © Illustrations Alison Carney 1999

The moral right of the author has been asserted
A CIP catalogue record of this book is available from the
British Library

ISBN 0 7475 4245 7

Printed in England by Clays Ltd, St Ives plc

10 9 8 7 6 5 4 3

Contents

Introduction

Learning to read with phonics is now recognised as one of the best ways in which a child can gain reading skills. The phonic system is not only used in most primary schools, but is also a method of teaching encouraged by the government, who recognise that the phonics method is a reliable and thorough way to teach reading.

Created to complement phonic reading in schools, this book is perfect for home reading. In its pages the young reader will find all the excitement and action they could want, as Pix and Pax enjoy mad-cap adventures with lots of fun and humour. Most importantly, the exciting story-line with controlled phonic vocabulary, will ensure that the beginner reader will soon be reading with confidence.

Meet the Cats

Pix and Pax are garden cats.
Pix is a fit cat. A get up to
tricks cat. He is a thin and trim
cat. Pix likes a small dish of
fish. That is all. Pax is a fat
cat. A sit on the mat cat. A nap
in your lap cat. Pax is always

in the mood for food. She will
eat anything, anytime,
anywhere.

Pix and Pax are garden cats.
The garden belongs to Fred. At
the bottom of the garden is a

long pond. Bob the frog lives in
the pond. He likes to hop in
and have a swim. Pix and Pax
do not like the water in the
pond.

Here is Gail. Gail is a snail.
Gail moves very, very slowly.
In a line behind Gail is a trail
of slime.

In the tall tree you can see Betty Bird. She always has a word to say. She tells everyone what to do. What a bossy old bird!

Today the grass is green. The sky is blue. What are the garden cats going to do?

Chapter One

It is a lazy summer day. The sun is burning high in the sky. It is so hot, that everything in the garden is melting. Even the bees are too hot to buzz. Only

Bob the frog is happy, splashing in his pond.

Pix and Pax are lying under the tree, trying to keep cool.

'I need a cold drink,' pants Pix.

'Me too,' says Pax, 'but I am too hot to move.'

'I wish that I could take my fur off,' Pix groans, as he rolls over, trying to find some cool ground.

'Try not to move,' says Pax, 'you will be cooler that way.'

Warm air wafts over the cats and they close their eyes sleepily. They keep very still. Pix is dreaming about chasing mice. Pax is dreaming about eating a big dish of fish. Then all of a sudden . . .

'WOOF WOOF WOOF!'

A big dog bounces into the garden.

'Go on, Zak,' says Fred. 'You play out here.'

Fred and his new friend Bill, go inside to have a cold drink. Pix and Pax jump up at once. All the fur stands up on their

backs. The cats do NOT like
dogs.

'WOOF,' says Zak, running
to the bottom of the tree.

The cats turn and flee. They
run up the tree trunk and on to
the wall. The wall is tall. Zak

jumps up, but he cannot reach the top of the wall.

'Go away dog,' hisses Pix.

'Go away dog,' hisses Pax.

'I only want to play,' barks Zak.

'Go and play somewhere
else,' say the cats. 'We do not
like dogs at all.'

Zak turns away. He sees
Betty standing in the middle of
the grass. She is pulling out a
worm for her dinner. Zak
rushes over to her.

'WOOF,' barks Zak. 'Will
you play with me?'

Betty flaps her wings and
flies up into the tree.

'Go away dog,' she chirps.
'You are too big to play with
me.'

Zak rushes around the

garden. Pix and Pax watch him from the top of the wall.

'WOOF,' he barks to Gail.

Gail does not like dogs. She curls up in a ball, inside her shell. She will not speak to Zak.

Zak runs over to the pond.

Bob is sitting on a log. Zak
sniffs the frog with his shiny
black nose.

'Go away you horrid dog,'
says Bob, and with a splash, he
plops into the pond.

Zak sits down. He is feeling
sad.

'I only wanted to have some fun,' he says.

From the top of the wall, Pix and Pax sniff. Fun with a dog! That cannot be!

Chapter Two

Dee comes out of Number
Three. Dee sees Pix and Pax
sitting on her wall. Dee does
not like cats. She does not like
them at all. She picks up a
broom.

'Scat cats!' she shouts, and

she pushes them with her broom.

Pix and Pax fall off the wall. 'Help!' they yelp.

Zak is under the wall. OH NO! Pix and Pax land on top of Zak's back. Their claws dig into Zak's back.

'ARGH!' screams Zak. He is under attack.

Zak leaps up and runs away. His tail wags and his ears flop madly. Pix and Pax pick

29

themselves up and run away
too.

Betty is on the grass. She sees
two mad cats and a mad dog
running towards her. She flaps
her wings and bats Zak on the
nose. Just then, Zak slips on a
trail of Gail's slime. He slips

and slides and cannot stop
himself. With one last bark, he
skids into Bob's pond.
SPLASH!

Zak sits up. His ears are wet.
His nose is wetter. Weeds are
dripping from his head. He
looks a sorry sight.

Pix stops. Pax stops. Betty stops. Gail peeps out of her shell. Bob leaps up on to his rock. He looks at Zak. Then he laughs.

'What a soppy dog,' he says.

Everyone sees how funny Zak looks.

Pix laughs. Pax giggles. Betty titters. And Gail sniggers. Zak looks at everyone. Then he laughs too.

'That was good fun,' says Pix.

'Yes,' agrees Pax. 'That was very good fun.'

'Can I be your friend?' asks

Zak. 'We could play some more fun games, until I have to go home.'

The garden cats agree. Zak leaps out of the pond.

'Oh goody, goody,' he says. He gives himself a great

shake. Water sprays everywhere.
Pix and Pax are soaked. They
do not like water at all, and
they do not like having a
shower.

'Not THAT game,' the cats
say crossly.

Bob, Betty and Gail laugh at the wet cats.

'Oh well,' says Zak, 'now you are two cool cats!'

Chapter Three

Dee at Number Three is in a bad mood. She sees Pax walking across her grass.

'Drat you cat,' she calls after Pax.

Pax walks past with her nose in the air. Dee picks up a

flowerpot and throws it at Pax,
but Pax jumps up the wall and
out of the way. The flowerpot
smashes into tiny bits.

Dee runs to see Fred.

'Keep that cat away from me,' she says crossly.

'I am sorry,' says Fred, stroking Pax's ears.

'Drat those cats,' Dee mutters

to herself, as she sweeps up the mess. 'Drat them with their fur on my dress. Drat them with their fishy smells and double drat them with their claws scratching my legs.'

Dee was being silly, because Pix and Pax did not go into Number Three very often. They never rubbed against Dee's legs. They never ate fish in her garden and they never got near

enough to scratch her. But Dee
doesn't like cats. She does not
like them at all.

Dee puts down her broom.
She wants a nice, quiet sit down.

Dee takes a comfy chair out of
her shed and puts it in the sun.
She gets out her book, her dark
glasses and her sun-hat.

Next door, Pix and Betty are

playing a game of tag, in the
garden. Pix is chasing Betty,
but Betty flies over the wall. Pix
jumps after her and leaps over
the wall. He lands SPLAT in
Dee's lap.

'AARGH!' shrieks Dee.

She drops her book and her
hat.

'You bad, bad cat,' she says
and she smacks Pix.

Pix runs away as fast as he
can.

'Fred!' she calls. 'You keep

those cats away from me.'

'I am sorry, Dee,' says Fred, scratching Pix's tummy.

Soon Dee is happy. There are no cats in her garden. She is having fun in the sun, when all of a sudden . . . two mice run over Dee's foot. Dee jumps up.

Her book goes flying. Her sun-hat falls off her head and her dark glasses whirl in the air.

'AARGH!' she screams. 'Help me!'

Fred comes running into Number Three. He sees Dee standing on her chair. She does not look at all happy now.

'What's wrong?' asks Fred.

'Please help!' says Dee. 'I don't feel very well.'

'What is the matter?' says Fred, rushing over.

'There are mice here,' whimpers Dee.

'Oh,' smiles Fred, 'well, I

think that I can help you there.'

Fred takes Dee home.

'You have a nice cup of tea,

Dee,' he says, 'and I will get rid of the mice for you.'

'Thank you so much,' says Dee, sinking into a chair.

Fred finds Pix and Pax. They are sleeping by the pond.

'Come along cats,' says Fred,
'I have got a job for you.'
But Pix and Pax don't want
to move. They don't like Dee

and they don't want to help
her.

Fred picks up the cats and
carries them into Dee's garden.

'Please,' he says, but the cats
stick their noses in the air.

They walk over to Dee's
doormat and curl up on it.
They do not want to help Dee.
Dee does not like cats and the
cats do not like Dee.

Fred goes back home. Pix and Pax open an eye. A blur flashes past. In the middle of the path, two mice stop. They sit up and twitch their noses.

Pix and Pax see them. The cats sit up at once. Pix and Pax do not like Dee, but two mice to chase – now THAT is good fun.

Pix and Pax freeze, only their eyes move, as they watch the two mice.

Slowly, they stalk the mice, treading softly and keeping low in the long grass. The mice do not even know that the cats are there.

Quickly, they pounce. The mice run. Pix jumps this way.

Pax jumps that way. The cats
chase the mice up and down,
round and round, until the mice
are dizzy.

At last, the mice run away,

out of the gate and down the
lane. Pix and Pax sit back and
lick their paws. That was great
fun!

'Well done!' says Fred.

'Yes,' says Dee, stroking the

cats. 'Thank you very much.'

Pix and Pax rub against
Dee's leg.

'Well,' says Dee to Fred,
'your cats don't leave fur on
my dress. They don't smell of
fish and they have not

scratched me. But they are
good at chasing away mice. Let
me give them a treat.'

So Dee goes into Number
Three and brings out a kipper.

Pix and Pax eat it all up.

'Perhaps,' says Dee, tickling them behind their ears, 'I do like cats after all.'

Pix and Pax purr happily.

OTHER YOUNG FICTION SERIES

CRAZY GANG (PHONIC READERS):
"Og Fo" Says the Space Bug
0 7475 3929 4 (hbk) / 3562 0 (pbk)
"Do I Look Funny To You?"
0 7475 3930 8 (hbk) / 3561 2 (pbk)
Pets Just Want to Have Fun
0 7475 3931 6 (hbk) / 3560 4 (pbk)
"I Don't Like Space Glop"
0 7475 3932 4 (hbk) / 3563 9 (pbk)
"Is That a Dog In the Sky?" 0 7475 4225 2 (pbk)
"This is Yum!" 0 7475 4230 9 (pbk)

Enjoy the zany mad-cap world of Max and Pat, and their
space friends Jazz and Zug-Zug, in these fun-filled books.
When Pat the dog and Zug-Zug the space bug meet, they
just want to have fun – but they can't help causing trouble!
Join Max and Jazz trying to keep an eye on their pets, and
having a crazy time along the way!

BEST PETS:
Timmy and Tiger 0 7475 3878 6 (hbk) / 3564 7 (pbk)
Gita and Goldie 0 7475 3879 4 (hbk) / 3656 5 (pbk)
Becky and Beauty 0 7475 3880 8 (hbk) / 3566 3 (pbk)
Paul and Percy 0 7475 3881 6 (hbk) / 3567 1 (pbk)

Your pet can be your best friend. Your pet will be loyal to
you, and look out for you. Sometimes your pet can even
save you from danger . . . In these heartwarming stories,
Tiger the cat, Goldie the dog, Beauty the pony and Percy
the parrot, prove that they really are best pets!